RAZORBILL

An imprint of Penguin Random House LLC, New York

First published in the United States of America by Razorbill, an imprint of Penguin Random House LLC, 2022

Visit us online at penguinrandomhouse.com.

Library of Congress Cataloging-in-Publication Data is available.

ISBN 9780593352076

Printed in the United States of America

1 3 5 7 9 10 8 6 4 2

PC

Design by Kristin Boyle
Text set in Gazette

BY INTERNATIONAL MUSIC STAR
KEVIN JONAS &
DANIELLE JONAS

THERE'S A ROCK CONCERT IN MY BEDROOM

ILLUSTRATED BY
COURTNEY DAWSON

RAZORBILL

Emma loves music.
She loves the

boom boom boom

of a good bass beat.

She loves the
her feet make when she dances.

STAMP STOMP STOMP!

And she loves to rock out with her mom,
her dad,
and her little sister.

Emma's learning to play the guitar.
Every day, her dad sits down with her
and they play together.

It's not perfect, but Emma knows she's getting better.

So when the sign goes up at school . . .
Emma knows just what she'll do.

Emma practices hard.
She works on her finger placement.

She works on her form.

And she learns a new song every night.

Emma's getting better and better. She can't wait for the big show! Her classmates are excited too.

Luis brags about all the tricks his dog is learning. "I'm basically a lion tamer."

Jamila's gymnastics practice is going great. "I'm thinking of trying out for the Olympic team."

Wendy guesses the right card every time.
"I should be on *America's Got Talent*."

Emma's heart sinks.
Compared to lion taming, Olympic tumbling, and actual
magic ... Well, playing the guitar doesn't seem very special.

"Everyone else is amazing and I'm totally ordinary,"
she tells her sister after school.
"What you have," Bella says, "is the jitters."

"What you need," Bella says, "is a lucky charm."
"Thank you," Emma says.

Having the lucky charm makes Emma feel braver.

"I'm learning to totally shred," she tells Luis, Jamila, and Wendy.

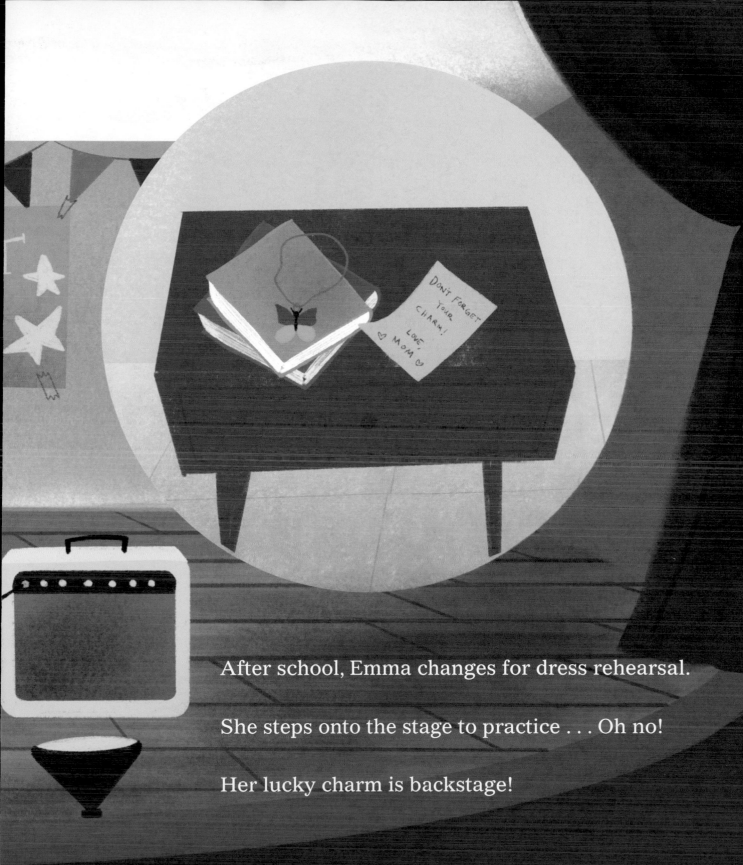

After school, Emma changes for dress rehearsal.

She steps onto the stage to practice . . . Oh no!

Her lucky charm is backstage!

Emma's hands are sweating.
Her fingers are shaking.
Her brain is buzzing,
and her heart is pounding.

Dress rehearsal is a disaster.

"I'm quitting the talent show!"

"But you love music," Emma's mom says.

"And you're getting so good at guitar!" her dad says.

"You're the star of our family dance parties," adds Bella. "Why shouldn't you be the star of the talent show?"

Emma does love music. She loves her guitar. And she loves their family dance parties.

But she doesn't love how her hands sweated. How her fingers shook. How her brain buzzed and her heart pounded.

"I wish," says Emma, "that being on stage felt as good as a family dance party."

"Hmm, I think we can make that happen," says Mom.

So Mom gets her dress rack.

Dad gets some pots and pans.

Bella finds an audience,
and then it's time to ROCK!

It's not a real show. But it feels like one.

STRUMMM

TWAAANG

THRUMMM

Emma's still kind of nervous, but she hits every note.

And with her family behind her…she could be a star.

The next night, at the talent show, Emma clutches her lucky charm. She thinks about her family dance parties. She takes a deep breath. And she steps out onto the stage.

Emma hits every note.

And with her family in front of her